The Horror From The Sea

By Matt Kirkby

Copyright 2012 Matt Kirkby
Draft2Digitial Edition

Draft2Digital Edition, License Notes
This book is licensed for your personal enjoyment only. This book may not be re-sold or given away to other people. If you would like to share this book with another person, please purchase an additional copy for each recipient. If you're reading this book and did not purchase it, or it was not purchased for your use only, then please return to Smashwords.com and purchase your own copy. Thank you for respecting the hard work of this author.

Chapter One

The low waves splashed softly against the white sand.

Lily squinted, raising her hand to shield her eyes from the bright tropical sunlight. The late morning sun felt wonderful on her bare skin. Her black and red bikini was skimpy enough to give her a good tan, while still being sufficiently modest for public viewing. "It's a real paradise here."

"That's just what the brochure said." Simon walked out onto the sand towards her. He was wearing a pair of swim trunks and loose short-sleeved shirt, unbuttoned to expose his muscular chest. When he reached her side, he stopped to look around. The water stretched to the horizon and beyond, the white sand curved gently around the cove, its edges lost behind the tropical foliage. "You can almost see Australia from here."

"Almost," Lily agreed. She gave the brightly coloured towel in her hand a vigorous shake and then laid it out on the sand. "It looks so much nicer now. Last night, it was really almost too dark to see anything."

Simon rested his hand on her shoulder. "We were lucky that the boat made it all the way here. When the engine died, I thought we'd have to row ourselves all the way back to the mainland." He chuckled loudly at that joke.

Lily glanced up at him. She had seen him in his tight swim trunks often enough that she was able to keep her attention on his face. Well, for most of the time. *He does look good in those trunks,* she thought. *Damn good.* Simon wasn't the least bit shy about taking his shirt off and enjoying the sun. "I don't think we'd have gotten very far rowing," she told him in a suddenly icy tone. "Not enough able-bodied men."

Simon chuckled at her. "Just me, the ship's captain, and his two crewmen. Yep, it would have been a long row for us. A real three hour tour." He began humming an old television theme song.

Lily sighed. He was obviously in no mood to take anything seriously. She looked back towards the resort.

A jungle-covered mountain rose up behind the hotel, forming a picturesque backdrop for the two story structure. The red tile roof glittered in the sun and the white stucco walls practically glowed. The second floor rooms all had balconies.

And no one out on any of them. Lily twisted her head for a better look at the rest of Orpheus Island again. "Oh Simon," she sighed. "The sand, the sea, the palms. This is just what I needed. To come out here and get away from it all."

"You're near enough a thousand miles away from civilization and any adoring fans."

Lily laughed. "I don't miss my fans," she said, still giggling. "Not all that much anyway. Oh, what's that?"

Simon squinted. "Looks like a crab."

"It's looks awfully big." The red shell on its back was easily the size of her foot. Lily made sure to take a careful step further away. "Do they usually grow this big?"

Simon laughed at the sound of concern in her voice. "Don't worry your pretty head about it. It's a lot more afraid of you than you are of it."

"You're a lot of help."

"You want me to protect you from the nasty sea creature?" Simon stepped closer to her hand began to massage her shoulders. "Just relax...that's why we're here."

"I know."

Laughter rose from further down the beach.

Lily glanced in that direction. A young blonde woman and her boyfriend were standing in the shallows, kicking water at each other and laughing loudly.

Simon's hands had stopped moving.

"Don't stare so much, Simon. You're drooling."

He leaned forward, pressing his body against her back.

She turned her head to look back at him. She could feel his chest against her back. *And if I lean further back, I bed I'd find something else to press against me.*

"I was just picturing you in that bikini."

"Is *that* what that rag is?" Lily sniffed and glanced back at the other couple. "I thought it was a face cloth she'd borrowed from the hotel. Anyway, purple is just not my colour."

"Don't be jealous. You'd look every bit as hot in it as she does."

"Shut up while you're ahead, dear." Lily turned back towards the ocean.

Simon chuckled again. "I am going for a swim," he announced. He pulled off his shirt and tossed it onto the sand.

"Have fun." Lily sat down on the towel. She glanced over her shoulder, but the crab had scuttled away and vanished. She adjusted her hat, so that it shaded her eyes, and then lay back.

With a shrug, Simon waded out into the waves.

Lily glanced out from under her hat.

The waves splashed against Simon's legs and soaked his swim trunks. The nylon clung tightly to him, showing off his hardness.

"Mmmm," Lily sighed.

* * *

The night breeze was cooling after the heat of the day. It carried the heavy salty scent of the ocean with it through the windows into the restaurant.

Lily walked through the doorway, with Simon in tow. She was dressed in a low-cut red blouse and black skirt. He was wearing tan cotton pants and a blue-green stripped shirt.

"I'll get us a table." Simon gave her a warm smile. "Or do you want to visit the bar first?"

She glanced towards the bar. The blond bartender was polishing glasses—he was looking towards her and had a big friendly smile on his face. "I'll bring something back for you," she told him. She walked away from the doorway, leaving Simon behind.

The restaurant wasn't overly crowded. There was seating for thirty or more...and less than a dozen patrons. A few elderly couples, a lot of young ones. None of them were paying any attention to her.

"Well, I wanted to be a no one again,"she murmured to herself. *I got my wish.* It made a change though. There was something liberating in being away from the crowds of adoring supposed fans and hangers on. *Life in L.A. can get just get so tiresome.*

One table had a tall Italian man. His greying hair was thick and curly, matching the hair showing through his partially unbuttoned shirt. His two companions were young women, both of whom looked young enough to be his daughters.

An elderly couple were seated at a second table. They had a bottle of wine between them and were talking softly.

"Good evening, Miss York."

Lily turned at the greeting. "Hello, Michelle. I didn't see you there."

Michelle Flannigan gave her a broad smile. She was wearing a loose sarong-style dress, showing off her tanned shoulders and the gentle curves of her breasts. She had styled her short brown hair into a spiky hairstyle. "I hope you and your friend are enjoying yourselves so far."

"Oh, we are," Lily told her. "We spent most of the day down on the beach and it was wonderful. I worked on my tan...and then Simon talked me into a going for a swim. The water was so warm. I hated to leave it."

"It will still be there tomorrow."

"A whole week of enjoying it...I can hardly wait. Your resort is even nicer than the pictures on your the website."

Michelle chuckled. "That's mostly Shelia's doing."

"You both manage a lovely resort." Lily glanced over her shoulder—she could see Simon already seated in a corner booth and looking a bit bored. He waved to them. "I should get Simon his drink."

"I'll bring your menus to your table. Unless you already know what you want. And judging from the man at your table, I'd wager you *do* know *exactly* what you want." Michelle gave her a wink and then walked away.

Lily was still smiling as she turned back towards the bar. She and Simon had first met Michelle and Shelia when they arrived at the resort the night before. The two owners had been friendly and happy to meet their newest guests.

Lily made her way slowly around the tables. She took the chance to glance at the other patrons. She didn't know anyone there—it was a relief to get away from Hollywood and seeing the same faces all the time—nor had she been introduced. *'Being able to just relax for a week without autograph seekers hanging around will be worth the long flight,'* she had told Simon.

The bartender looked up and smiled. He was the iconic Aussie surfer—bronzed skin, with sun-bleached hair and bright green eyes. "Evening, miss," he said. "What can I get you?"

Lily loved the sound of his Australian accent. "I'd like two drinks."

"Are you that serious a drinker?" He laughed then, his amusement making his eyes twinkle.

"Hardly. I'll take a rum-and-coke for my friend...and I think I'd like to have sex-on-the-beach."

"I bet you would," he replied with a leer.

"That's not your usual drink," a deep voice interjected.

Lily's smile faded from her face. Taking a deep breath, she turned around so that she was looking at the speaker. "Ivan. I had no idea that you would be vacationing here."

Ivan walked past her and sat down on one of the bar stools. His pale blue cotton shirt was loose on his torso, partially unbuttoned so that it hung open halfway down his hairy chest to catch the cooling breeze. "Lily York." He gave her a twisted smile. "Fancy meeting you way out here."

Lily brushed her red hair away from her eyes. She did not return his smile. She ignored his open shirt and his tanned, hairy chest as well, keeping her gaze on his face.

"Your usual, Ivan?"

"Yes, thank you, Jamie." Ivan picked up the rum-and-coke from the bartender. The ice cubes in the glass clinked softly as he lifted it to his lips.

"What the hell are you doing here?" Lily demanded

Ivan grinned at her. "Having a drink and enjoying myself. You should try it sometime."

She sniffed. "I came here to relax...not to meet up with you again."

"I wasn't looking for you either."

"Good for that then." Lily turned away from him and looked down at the bar.

Jamie gave her a sheepish shrug and went back to mixing her second drink. "That was my drink you just took."

Ivan raised the glass in a toast. "Thank you."

Lily bristled. "I see that you haven't changed."

"Not one little bit. I'm still the same charming rogue you used to meet up with in seedy motel rooms."

"You certainly wouldn't go anywhere classy."

Jamie set a second run-and-coke onto the bar, next to her own mixed drink. "Here you go, miss." He glanced towards Ivan.

He held up his glass again and gave her a grin. "Bottoms up."

"Enjoy your drink, Ivan." She picked up the two glasses and then paced across the restaurant, past the other tables, towards the booth where Simon was sitting. He had his face buried behind a menu.

"Excuse me."

Lily stopped at the soft voice and turned around. "Yes?"

The blonde from the beach had traded in her purple bikini for a more modest top and short black mini-skirt. "I hate to bother you, but aren't you Lily York?"

"Why, yes, I am." Lily pasted a friendly smile on her face.

"I'm a huge fan of yours. Betty Randal." She offered her hand.

Lily set the drinks down onto the table so she could return the shake. Simon was still hidden behind his menu.

"I hate to be a pain, but could I have your autograph?" Betty asked.

"Of course."

"Thank you again." Betty hastily began digging through her pockets. "I must have a pen on me."

"I always carry one." Simon handed her one from behind his menu. "Here."

Lily took it and a napkin. She quickly scrawled a brief message and then signed her name. "Here you go, Betty."

"Thank you ever so much." Betty gave her an eager smile. "I never dreamed that I would be staying at the same resort as you. Donny is going to be so jealous. My boyfriend tells me that I'm as pretty as you are, but I don't believe him. You're simply stunning."

"Thank you." Lily sat down at her table and watched Betty hurry back to her table.

Simon chuckled, then peaked out from behind the menu. "So much for being a thousand miles away from your fans."

"Shut up."

"Are you always this bitchy when you're on vacation?"

"Only when I run into annoying men." She took a long swallow from her drink, then picked up the menu and skimmed the list of specialities. There was a good selection.

"Which man?" Simon had lowered his menu and was now scanning the handful of other patrons. "There's not a lot to choose from."

"It doesn't matter."

Simon narrowed his eyes. "You're upset. I think it matters."

"It doesn't." Lily lifted her head as the waitress approached. "I'll have the seared scallops," she said. "And another drink. Sex-on-beach." She drained her glass. "I am not thinking about him. We're here to relax, Simon."

"If you say so."

"I do." She gave him a warm smile. "So tell me how much you're enjoying yourself."

Chapter Two

Ivan let the door swing closed behind him. He walked away from the restaurant, heading towards the sandy path which led back to his cabin. The night breeze was blowing off the ocean and it did feel nice and cooling after the heat of the day. His head was spinning—and not from too much drinking. For a change. He hadn't enjoyed the evening. Not since *that woman* had walked into the restaurant.

Jamie had noticed his mood—his second rum-and-coke had been twice as strong as normal—but had not said anything.

Michelle had noticed the exchange and had come to sat down beside him for a bit, as well, and asked how he knew Lily York.

'I worked with her back in Hollywood,' he'd replied with a sour twist on his lips. *'Before she became the Ice Queen.'*

'She seems quite nice.'

'Don't be fooled. It's all an act.'

'She can't be that bad.'

'She is.'

'Well, she's staying here for the next week. Just so you know.'

"I should just stay away for the next week," he muttered to himself. "I could stay in my cabin and—no, screw that! I'm not gonna hide away just because she's here." He stumbled over a rock and cursed out loud. *Michelle should have this path cleaned up better.* "Or I could do it for her."

A small red-shelled crab scuttled past his foot.

He kept walking.

And brooding about Lily. She was such a phoney. She had played a role in the restaurant—that of *'woman in love'*--just like she always did. *In love with herself,* he thought. *Did she think she was performing in front of an audience?* Leaning in close to her boyfriend of the week, giggling at every word he said, feeding him bites of food from her own plate. It was all quite nauseating.

He snorted. "And the award for best actress goes to—"

"Now, isn't this nice?"

Ivan froze in his tracks as a man's voice spoke loudly. He looked around, his eyes wide in the moonlight, but he didn't see anyone.

A woman giggled. "Oh you...."

Squinting in the direction of the voice, Ivan took a step off the sandy path and pushed a few hibiscus branches aside.

A blonde woman stood in a small clearing, leaning up against a tree. A young man had his hands wrapped around her waist and his lips were on her neck.

Ivan sighed softly. *I remember when I used to hold Lily like that.* He gave himself a mental shake.

The man lifted his face away from her neck. "I love you, Betty."

"I know, Donny." She pulled away from him, giving herself a little twirl as she did so. Her black skirt swirled around her legs. "I feel a bit dizzy. The night air just isn't clearing my head."

"It isn't?" Donny laughed softly.

"I should have stopped at three glasses of wine. No matter what you said about being on vacation. I think you're trying to get me drunk." She giggled.

"Yep, that was my plan. Get you drunk and then I can take full advantage of you right here and now." Donny moved close and grabbed her waist again.

"Oh stop!" she protested, still giggling. "Someone will see us!"

"Who?" Donny asked with a laugh of his own. "The resort is more than half empty. There's no around to see us...and everyone else is here for the same reason we are. Romance." He kissed her again. "Passion." His hand gripped her breast. "Sex."

Betty giggled.

Donny lifted up her top, sliding his hands under the cotton so that he could cup her breasts.

Betty closed her eyes and sighed.

Donny pulled down her skirt and her panties, sliding the material down past her knees. "Just step out of them," he said.

Betty's hands were fumbling with the belt on his shorts.

Ah, young love. Ivan turned to leave as the young couple sank down into the sand. He shouldn't be standing there, spying on them. *I really should have learned my lesson that time Lily and I got caught by the river....*

* * *

Lily stood on the balcony and inhaled deeply. The night air around the resort was still heavy with the fragrance of hibiscus, bougainvillea, and poinciana. "What the hell is that?"

The ground itself appeared to be moving.

Simon stepped out of their room and onto the balcony. He had stripped down to his boxer shorts, careless of any potential watchers. "What are you looking at?" he asked.

"Shouldn't you put some clothes on?" she asked. The moonlight was playing off his body, the silk of his shorts only just hiding his manhood. "Someone might see—"

"See what? These are perfectly acceptable for public viewing. No worse than some of the swimsuits around here. I mean, did you see what that old guy was wearing? Only an Italian would try to get away with a thong *Speedo*." Simon reached for her arm and pulled her close. "Anyway, it's dark. Who can see anything?"

"I guess."

"We're not in Hollywood. Not anywhere near Hollywood." Simon rubbed her shoulders. "There aren't any paparazzi lurking in the bushes."

Lily had gone back to staring down at the ground.

"What are you looking at?"

"The ground...."

"What's so special about the ground?" Simon leaned over the balcony railing. "Crabs? Are those *crabs*?" he asked in confusion.

"There must be hundreds of them down there."

"Thousands." Simon shook his head. "I've never seen so many in one place before."

The living carpet covered the ground, stretching as far as the eye could see, as hundreds of thousands of crabs scuttled from the ocean across the sand and into the forest.

"Are they dangerous?"

"Course not." Simon spat. "Might get a nasty little pinch from one, but they're hardly dangerous."

"I'm glad we're up here."

"I'm sure there's nothing to worry about. Probably just some annual migration. Can't be all that serious—there's nothing in the brochure about it."

"The resort is open year round, except for one weekend in March when the hotel grounds are buried beneath a living carpet of crabs." Lily giggled at the absurdity of it.

Simon gave her arm a gentle squeeze. "Come along to bed."

"Right now?"

"Yes, right now." Simon gave her a grin. "Unless you have something else that you'd rather be doing."

"No, I think my appointment book is clear." Lily followed Simon back through the door and into their hotel room. "At least for a bit."

"Good to know that you can still squeeze me in."

She reached out and let her fingers run down his chest, across his stomach, and then down inside his boxer shorts. "I can *squeeze* something," she said and he gasped.

"Come over here!" He pulled her down onto the bed. "I think," he kissed her mouth, "that you," he kissed her again, "are seriously overdressed."

"It's just a nightie."

"It's still too much."

"It's still too much."

Chapter Three

"Did you see all those crabs last night?"

"What was that, Ivan?" Shelia had a fine Australian twang to her voice. She had a tall drink sitting in front of her, complete with a pink paper umbrella, and an abandoned paperback beside it on the table. She turned her head enough so that she could look at Ivan. "What crabs?"

Ivan put his plate and glass onto the table and sat down sat down in an empty chair. The handful of other patrons in the restaurant were eating quietly, and most of their plates were now empty. Shelia had chosen a table at the back of the room—she could see every table in the place, and be seen in turn, but she was dining alone. *Well, until I came along,* Ivan thought. "A whole horde went past us last night. I stood on my deck and watched them scuttling by. Must have been hundreds of the things. Maybe thousands."

"Going off on their way to spawn, I dare think."

"Crossing overland from the ocean to the lagoon?"

"They migrate. Most living creatures do." Shelia reached for her drink and took a sip. "*You* migrated here after all."

"I wanted to get away from things. I'd had enough of people."

"So you chose to stay at a busy resort?"

"It's not that busy." There might have been a dozen people booked in right now. *She's got room for a hundred guests or more, but I've never seen the place that busy.* Just a single couple were still at one of the tables, lingering over their breakfast.

"It's busy enough." She charged good rates for staying on the island and her resort's service—and the natural beauty of Orpheus Island—was good enough that guests were willing to pay. "We opened this place on a dream I'll have you know."

"Glad to see that it wasn't a nightmare." Ivan reached for the plate of cut fruit he had brought with him. "Michelle and I go way back you know. I've known her for years."

"Since your childhood when you used to vacation in Sidney. She's spoken of you often enough, before you moved out here." Shelia nodded her head. "Sometimes she just rambles on and on about the most boring subjects."

Ivan shrugged. "Glad to know I keep the two of you amused," he said around a mouthful of pineapple.

"And too think," Sheila said as she picked up her drink, "we chose to build out our dream resort on this island to avoid the riffraff."

"You don't own the whole island."

"We own most of it, mate."

"And you charge a good rent even for just a small cottage." Ivan chuckled. *It was a price I'm more than willing to pay though.* The island was beautiful and it was peaceful. *They don't generally cater to families so there aren't any packs of screaming kids running around. No* ankle-biters *here, as Shelia would say.*

Shelia laughed. "It's not that much in rent. A pittance compared to what we could charge a *guest.*"

"True," he admitted. He took a bite from an orange slice. "Even with cheap rent, you still get the better of this deal."

"How so? I could make three months of what you pay rent in just *one* week if I had real guests staying there."

"Yes, but I rely on your resort for most of my food and entertainment. You make good money off me that way."

"And we get to be featured as characters in your various novels." Shelia set the empty glass back onto the table. "I am not sure that I like the idea of publicity in pages of your smutty ideas."

"My books are classy."

Shelia chuckled. "So you say."

"Have you even bothered sitting down to actually read any of my books?"

"Maybe I prefer smutty."

They both laughed.

Shelia stood up and carried her glass back towards the bar. "I need a refill."

The restaurant door swung open.

Shelia kepet walking forwards, with a friendly smile on her face as one of her guests stepped through. "G'day, Miss."

Lily was wearing a low-cut top and shorts. They flattered her figure and showed off how well her new tan was coming. "Good morning, Shelia."

"Just you this morning?"

"Simon is still sleeping." Lily took an idle look around the restaurant. "It's not very busy this morning."

"You missed most of the rush."

"And *good morning* to you too, Ivan."

"Good morning, Miss York." He gave her a pleasant smile, to take the sting from his mocking tone. "Have a seat and join us."

"Oh, I'd hate to intrude."

"It's no intrusion." Shelia gestured to one of the seats. "I'll have Jamie whip you up a nice drink. Something sweet and tropical to get the blood flowing."

"Sure. I'm on vacation...might as well be adventurous."

"That's the spirit. I'll be right back." Shelia walked towards the bar.

Lily sat down.

Ivan was seated across from her, slowly sipping a pale orange drink. Ice clinked in his glass as he set it back down on the table. "I don't recall you ever really being the adventurous type."

"People change," she replied.

"So they do. Are you happy to be here?"

"Of course I am." Lily nodded her head. "It's nice to just get away for a rest."

"Must be a challenge

Lily watched the young couple hurry past and head outside. "Young love," she sighed.

"When did you get old?" Ivan countered.

"After I hooked up with some crusty washed up author."

Ivan snorted at that.

Lily looked at him. "What are you doing here?"

"Finishing my breakfast."

"No, I mean why are you here? On Orpheus island?"

"Because I like the weather. The temperature is warm, the sea breeze is refreshing, the landscape is amazing."

"You could get that anywhere just about anywhere. Back in L.A."

"There are a hell of a lot fewer agents and actresses here."

"No journos nor posties either," a woman's voice added.

"Hello, Jasmine." Ivan pushed his empty plate away.

"Good morning, Ivan." Jasmine gave him a warm smile. She had to be pushing the other side of sixty, but she was a hard worker and usually left Shelia and Michelle amazed at how quickly she looked after the various rooms in the resort. In the busy season, she'd have a staff under her, but with things so slow right now, she was the only maid currently working.

"Are you our waitress today?"

"Mz Cooke asked me to bring this to the young lady." Jasmine set a glass containing a pinky and frothy liquid onto the table in front of Lily. "You should enjoy this. It's one of Jamie's personal creations."

Lily eyed it.

"It should be safe," Ivan told her. "Jamie has never poisoned anyone."

"Shut your gob," Jasmine told him. "Can I bring you a breakfast menu?"

"No, I'll just have some scrambled eggs and toast."

"That we can do." Jasmine gave her a friendly smile. "Would you like anything else, Ivan?"

"No, I'm good."

"I'll leave the two to your conversation then." Jasmine turned and shuffled away.

* * *

"That water looks nice and refreshing," Simon commented. Low waves were splashing gently against the sand.

"Yes, it does." Lily nodded her head. The sea matched the sky for sheer overwhelming blueness. She was wearing a two-piece swimsuit, still working on her tan. "It's getting quite warm."

Simon sat upright in his beach chair. "Let's go for a dip."

"What?"

"Let's go in for a dip. It'll cool us both off." Simon stood up. He pulled his tee-shirt over his head and tossed it carelessly onto the closest beach chair.

"Well, I don't—"

"Come on. Don't be such an old woman."

Lily followed him to the water. The sand was hot on her bare feet, but the water felt lovely and cool as the first waves splashed up to her knees. "Oh, this does feel nice."

"Told you." Simon pulled her deeper into the water.

Lily closed her eyes as she waded out. The water rose to her waist.

"You look relaxed."

"I feel so...bare." Her eyes snapped open. "What the hell are you doing?" she demanded.

Simon was stuffing her bikini top into the pocket of his trunks. "I'm just giving you some extra exposure." He chuckled. "Relax."

"Someone will see us!"

"So what? There's no one around. The island is practically deserted." He took her in his arms and hugged her. "Enjoy it."

Lily gasped as he spun her around, his hands cupping her breasts and gently massaging them. She leaned back against him, letting his muscular arms hold her as his fingers continued to play with her nipples, squeezing and pulling. As she gave him the full weight of her body, she realized that he had somehow managed to shove down his swim trunks and she could feel his hardness pressing against her thighs.

"Just relax," he crooned. "Don't think. Just enjoy the sun and the water and the feel of what I am doing to you." He slid one hand down her abdomen, lower and lower.

Lily giggled and shifted positions as the waves lapped against her.

Simon's fingers teased her.

"Uh," she moaned.

"That's right, let yourself go," Simon whispered.

"Take me," she said, no longer caring who might be watching. "Take me all the way."

Instead, Simon pulled back.

"Don't stop!" she pleaded. She half-turned. "Don't stop now!"

"Hang on."

She heard foil tearing and she twisted her head further back to look at him.

He was fumbling with something under the water.

Then he smiled and thrust himself forward.

She gasped aloud as he entered her. Somehow, he'd planned this encounter out well enough to bring a condom and put it on. She jerked, trying to pull away.

"Relax," Simon whispered as he wrapped his arms around her body. He held her tight against him. "Just let it happen."

"Oh, I am...." she sighed. He felt so good inside of her.

He began to move, rocking her with him, thrusting deeper.

She gasped, caught up in the emotions and heat of the moment.

Simon breathed more and more heavily. Then he cried out.

She raised her voice with him.

Simon slumped against her. "Damn, Lily, that was amazing."

"It was." She felt his firm grip on her shoulders, could feel him still within her. "Wow...that was intense." It wasn't like this in bed last night, she thought.

They stood in the ocean, still rocking gently, the softness of the waves lapping against their heated skin.

Ivan stepped away from the window and lowered his binoculars. "Be thankful that I don't have a camera with a telephoto lens," he muttered. "Otherwise your career would be in serious danger of over-exposure."

He walked to his computer and looked at the blank screen.

He needed to write something new and get it sent off

But his muse wasn't talking to him.

He moved back to the window and picked up the binoculars again.

Lily wasn't the only bikini-clad woman on the beach today. She was just one of four—though she was the prettiest, in his opinion—and he spent some time admiring the others.

"Just for character research," he told himself. "Purely for academic reasons." He was getting hard inside his shorts.

Chapter Four

"Isn't this just so romantic, Donny?"

"Yeah, sure." Donny stumbled over a half-buried rock and cursed softly.

"I've always wanted to make love on a beach by moonlight." Betty paused for a moment to stare at the moonlight rippling from the waves as they splashed against the beach.

Donny caught up to her. "You look really beautiful." He leaned in close so that he could kiss her.

"Are we far enough away?"

"I can't even see the hotel," Donny replied. "No one is gonna see us."

"Are you sure?"

"Course I am." He kissed her neck again. "Come on."

Betty returned his kiss.

His hands roamed up her arms, coming around her neck, and then drifting down to her chest.

Betty moaned as Donny's fingers undid her top and allowed it to fall open.

Betty reached down and unzipped his shorts. The denim slid down his legs and dropped around his ankles.

Donny stepped out of his shorts and pressed himself against her. "Come on," he whispered. "You can't stop now."

She could feel his hardness against her hot skin.

They sank down onto the sand, ignoring their discarded clothing.

The sand was still warm from the day's heat as the two young bodies rolled about in it. The air was heavy with the scent of hibiscus and bushes rustled.

Donny murmured softly as he kissed his way down her neck.

Betty winced, feeling something pull at her hair. "Not so hard," she whispered.

"Anything you say." Donny bent closer to her neck, nuzzling her.

Betty closed her eyes and leaned back to enjoy the sensations. Her boyfriend has been eager enough when she suggested they make love on the beach. Now they were both laying in the sand and he was nibbling at her neck and—"Ouch!"

"Ouch?" Donny pushed himself off of her. "What are—ow!"

Betty gave her foot a shake. "Ow!"

"What's going on?" Don pushed himself to his feet. "What the hell—"

The entire beach was moving.

"Crabs!" Betty gave a cry of fright.

Hundreds of them were swarming over the beach.

"What the hell!" Donny kicked at one, but there were countless others swarming around them to take its place.

"I'm bleeding!" Betty's tone was one of disbelief. "They're pinching me." She tried to back away, but there was no clear space for her to stand on. "Ow!"

Something bigger loomed out of the bushes.

Betty screamed.

Donny spun around. His feet were bloody and the crabs were scuttling around him. "What the hell?"

Claws reached for him.

* * *

"I just can't get over how quiet this whole place is," Lily York commented over breakfast. "You hardly ever see anyone around."

Simon picked up his coffee cup. "I know, Lily. We're isolated from pretty much everything out here. I can't even get a daily newspaper." He shrugged.

"That's one reason I like it here so much," Lily countered. "The privacy is a clear draw...not a single reporter within a thousand kilometres."

"Well, maybe not quite that far." Simon set his coffee mug back down onto the table. "We're not that far from the coast."

"We're far enough. Just you and me, a dozen or so other people, and an entire island." Lily sighed. "As close to a private paradise as we can get."

"I like places with more people. A little more action would suit me."

"You want to bar-hop? Don't you get enough of that back in L.A.?"

"It's my way of relaxing. There's not enough different faces around here."

Lily shook her head. "Have you see that young couple this morning?"

"What couple?"

Lily set her glass of pineapple juice down on the table. "The blonde and her surfer. You know."

"The one with the purple bikini?"

"I knew you'd remember *that* particular detail."

Simon grimaced. "You brought her up."

"I don't see her. Or him."

"Probably just sleeping in." He speared a piece of egg with his fork. "Why, afraid that I'm gonna go off and offer her a part in a movie?"

"No one would pay to see the types of movies you'd produce."

"Your words wound me, madam," Simon replied in an affected snobbish accent. "Wound me to the quick, I dare say."

"Hrmph," she sniffed.

* * *

Ivan leaned back in his office chair and stretched out his back. He stared blankly at the laptop monitor in front of him. The sea breeze was strong this morning.

"Blowing up a storm," he said aloud. "A pity it isn't blowing in some inspiration for me." An *Abba* CD was playing softly on the stereo in the background, but he had tuned the music out while he tried to concentrate. "I need fresh ideas...." Sometimes the perfect choice of words simply flowed out of him...and sometimes they simply did not.

He let out a sigh.

An entire day spent and he had less than half a thousand words to show for it. "What a waste of my time," he muttered. "How the hell am I supposed to pay the rent if I can't get anything written?"

Last week the words had tumbled out of his brain even faster than he could type them out...and they had all been perfect, hardly needing any editing.

This week, nothing.

"Fine." With a grunt, he turned off the computer and stood up. "I think I'll take an early supper. Maybe I can find some interesting conversation in the bar." He checked that everything was turned off—no sense in wasting the charge in the solar batteries—and then left his cottage to walk along the path towards the resort.

Simon was standing near the door to the restaurant. He was wearing tan pants and a loose shirt, with a Tilly hat on his head.

"Evening," Ivan said politely as he approached.

Simon was scowling at him. "Your presence upsets Lily."

Ivan blinked. "I beg your pardon?"

"Running into you has brought up a bunch of old memories. A lot of things she'd rather have remained buried." Simon's voice was cold. "Like how you betrayed her."

"Betrayed her? How, by packing up my stuff and leaving her the apartment? I never meant to hurt her," Ivan told the other man. "And for the record, *she* left *me.* If anyone should be upset—"

"I'd look on it as a personal favour if you would stay out in your cabin for the rest of the week."

"A favour." Ivan could barely believe that he had heard that offer.

"Yes..." Simon said, clearly trying to sound reasonable. "A simple enough request. Assuming that you ever want anyone in Hollywood to look at one of your scripts ever again."

Ivan's eyes narrowed. "Thank you for the advice." His voice had turned as cold as Simon's earlier tone.

A faint smirk was playing across Simon's face.

"Now take some of mine."

Simon's jaw dropped.

Ivan tapped his finger against Simon's chest. "What we had between us is all over and done with. Lily York means *nothing* to me. Absolutely nothing. If she's fucking you, then enjoy it while it lasts."

The other man's face was growing darker.

"I'm just here for my meals," Ivan told him. "And I have as much right to be here as you and your *girlfriend*." He allowed just a hint of pain to colour to his voice. "So maybe the two of you should think about making use of room service for the rest of the week." He pushed past Simon and pulled the door open so he could go inside.

Simon didn't try to stop him.

* * *

Simon felt a cool breeze blowing through the open balcony doors. He looked up as Lily emerged from the bathroom. She was wearing a loose silk robe which draped around her body. "Are you ready for bed yet?"

She shook her head. "I'm just not tired yet." She walked towards the balcony.

"You should be after today. All that fresh sea air...."

"And our cooling dip?" she asked.

Simon chuckled. "Yes, that too."

"Looks like a storm is blowing up. The moon is all wreathed with clouds." Lily was standing on the balcony. "They're everywhere!"

Simon blinked at her over the top of his *Kobo* ereader. "What are?"

"Those crabs."

Simon shook his head. He put his ereader down on the nightstand. "Come back to bed. You're still dreaming."

Lily shook her head. "I'm wide awake." She turned back towards the ground with the swarming crabs.

"Come on back to bed." Simon held out his arms. "I'm waiting for you."

Lily stepped back through the French doors and undid her bathrobe. A gust of wind caught the fabric and made it flap.

"Don't worry about the crabs out there." He held his hands, holding his fingers together like pincers. "Worry about me."

Giggling, she slipped between the sheets.

Chapter Five

Jamie paced along the corridor. His sleeveless orange tee-shirt was tight against his chest and his baggy shorts did nothing to hide his muscular legs. "Quite the storm last night."

"Yeah, it was." Ivan nodded as he stopped. The carpet was soft under his sandals, like the beach sand. The corridor was lined with doors, but none of the rooms in this wing were in currently use by any guests. "I had to clear a few branches away from the cabin. No damage, luckily, but a few came down."

"No harm around here."

"Good to hear. You taking some time off?"

"Yep," Jamie nodded. "Should be some good waves out there today. I've got some free time and I'm gonna go out and ride them."

"I've never been able to get the hang of riding a wave."

"It's like Zen. You just find your spot and away you go." Jamie grinned. "Just like landing a shelia."

"Just like that?" Ivan asked.

"Yep. There's always a few shelias around, looking to get some quiet time." Jamie brushed at the front of his t-shirt. "Always someone looking for a little harmless romance on her vacation."

"You know that Shelia doesn't like you hitting on her guests."

Jamie shrugged. "I don't hit on any of them. I just happen to provide lonely girls with company. The rest of the time, I just enjoy the scenery. I mean, did you see that blonde in the purple bikini the other day? She was hot."

"No, I didn't see her."

"She was on the beach most of yesterday. Came into the bar for lunch and I honestly don't know what was keeping her in that top. She must have been using tape." He shook his head. "But I haven't seen her today."

"Well, she must be around somewhere."

"Yeah. Maybe I'll see her when I'm out surfing."

"You could show her your board."

Jamie chuckled. "Yeah, that I could. I've got some moves she'd really enjoy."

Too be young again, Ivan thought with a grin.

Jamie gave himself a shake. "I should get going. I'm wasting waves."

"Have fun then."

"Always." Jamie continued on his way.

Ivan turned and kept walking down the corridor.

* * *

"I've got to take a leak."

"Oh, Simon, right here?" Lily exhaled heavily.

"Yeah. It's all those tropical drinks you keep getting for me."

"I never made you drink any of them," she replied irritably. "They were all your idea."

He gave her a slight grin and stepped off the path.

"Don't go too far."

"Yes, dear!" he called back.

She shook her head in resignation. "Simon, Simon, Simon." She stared up into the treetops as a brightly-coloured bird flew past to land on a branch. "I'm not going to stand here trying to bird watch for hours you know." She paced around, wandering a short distance away from the tree.

The bird squawked.

Lily eyed it, wondering what type of bird it was. *Parrot?* She shrugged. *Who really cares?* She paused and inhaled directly from a particularly large hibiscus. "Simon?"

There was no response.

Lily shook her head. "Did you forget how to work your fly?" she asked as she walked back towards the tree. "Are you waiting to re-enact that love scene from *Enter The Jungle Queen*? If so, forget it. I am *not* swinging down a vine wearing a leopard skin bikini. Well, not again, anyway." Frowning, she stepped around the tree. "Simon?"

The path was empty.

"How far away did you go?" she called out. "It's not like I haven't seen you taking a piss before."

Lily stopped. She had circled the tree twice.

"Simon?" she called out more loudly this time. "Simon?" She heard the panic in her voice and tried to take a few calming breaths. "He can't have gone too far, right?" She looked at the ground, but she could not see any obvious tracks. "I'm not a girl scout, I'm an actress." She was also talking to herself. "Simon!"

"What's wrong?" a man's voice asked.

"Simon is missing." Lily was so relieved to see another friendly face. Even if it was Ivan. "We were walking out here and he stepped off the path for a moment."

"Why?"

"Oh...no reason. Call of nature," she added, feeling her cheeks grow hot. "Anyway, he's gone."

Ivan scowled at her. "He can't have gone far. It's not that big of an island after all." He was wearing hiking boots and khaki shorts and his pale green shirt was hanging open, showing off his chest.

"Very funny." Lily took a few steps away from him. "He's probably hiding in the bushes, waiting to play some cruel trick on me."

Ivan shrugged. "Could be."

"I mean, if Simon had tripped or had fallen and was hurt, then he would have cried out. I would have heard him." Lily tried to keep panic from her voice.

"Probably." Ivan nodded his agreement, though he looked puzzled.

"So where the hell is he?"

"I'll help you look for him." Ivan stretched out his arms. "He might have had a coconut fall on his head or something."

"I hope not."

Ivan looked around at the ground as he paced around the tree. "It doesn't make much sense," he said. "Unless the two of you ha a fight and he just left you here."

"That's ridiculous. What would we fight about?"

"I can't imagine anyone wanting to get away from you," Ivan mocked.

Lily sniffed loudly. She turned and stalked up the path.

Ivan turned and pushed his way through a few hibiscus bushes. *I shouldn't have done that,* he thought. *It wasn't nice.*

Ivan froze.

There were a pair of feet sticking out from under a particularly bushy plant.

"What is it?" Lily called out. She hurried towards him.

"I think I found him."

Lily shook her head as she walked past Ivan and towards the bush. "Asleep, I should have guessed." She strode forward. "Get up, you lazy—" She moved the leaves aside with her foot.

Ivan came running as Lily's scream echoed through the jungle.

"What happened to him!" Lily was backing away, shaking. "What happened?"

Ivan moved the leaves aside with his hand. "Christ."

Most of the body was little more than bones now, covered with a just few scraps of bloody flesh.

"What happened to Simon!"

Ivan put his arms around her and pulled her away from the grisly sight. "Calming breaths," he said. "Take deep calming breaths."

"What the hell happened to him?"

"I don't know." Ivan kept his arms around her.

Chapter Six

Back at the resort, Lily was laid out on her bed, the sheets pulled up around her. She was breathing deeply, but softly. Her eyes were closed.

"I've given her a mild sedative." Michelle Flannigan closed up her bag and turned to the other two people present. "She should sleep the night through at least. Rest is the best thing we can do for her right now."

"This is horrible."

Ivan was sitting in one of the guest chairs and now he lifted his head to look at Shelia Cooke.

"How could this happen?" the resort manager continued in a low tone of voice. She had been sitting in a chair and mumbling under her breath for some time. "We've never had a guest eaten alive before."

"Some kind of animal." Ivan shrugged, uncertain of what could actually have killed Simon. He had never seen anything like that before. "Looks like a skeleton of a cow after it wandered into a river of piranha."

"There are no piranha around here. Wrong side of the ocean," Michelle said. "And you won't find any bloody piranha in the jungle."

"I know that," Ivan replied.

Shelia shook her head. "The investors will have a field day with this."

"Don't lose your head, dear. Remember your blood pressure." Michelle put her arm around Shelia. "You should go downstairs and have yourself a cuppa."

"That's your answer for everything!" Shelia countered shrilly. "'Go and put on a pot of tea.' 'Just take a cuppa.' 'I should go put the kettle on.' Well this little situation is beyond a cup of tea! How could this be happening?"

"We'll find out the answer," Michelle told her calmly.

Shelia blinked.

"You should go back downstairs and make yourself useful. You do have a number of other guests, right?"

"Of course," Shelia replied.

"Then go look after their needs. Keep yourself busy. In the meantime, I should go out and recover that body. Ivan, will you come and help us?"

"Of course." He nodded and stood up.

"We'll bring it—him—to my office." Michelle grimaced. "I guess. The surgery's just not designed to handle an autopsy."

"Autopsy?"

"Deep breaths, Shelia." Michelle sighed. "I thought I was done with all that kind of stuff after we left Sidney," she said in a low tone. "I was looking forward to being out here with nothing more serious to worry about than sunstroke. Strains on the tennis court. The occasional jellyfish sting. Not something like this."

Ivan followed her into the hallway. Shelia had already vanished from sight. He watched Michelle close and lock the door behind her. "So what caused this?"

"I don't know."

"But can you find out?"

"I hope so." Michelle shook her head. "This is the worst accident to ever happen here."

"We'll get through it." Ivan tried to sound cheerful. "Don't worry."

* * *

Hours later, Ivan was sitting at the bar nursing his drink when Michelle walked into the restaurant and sat down beside him. He kept staring at his drink.

"How many of those have you had?"

"This is my first glass." Ivan looked up with bleary eyes. "Of course, Jamie has refilled it five or six times."

Michelle sat down on a bar stool. "I'll have the same," she announced loudly. "Make it a double, Jamie."

Jamie nodded, not saying a word. He hurried to the other end of the bar.

Ivan took another sip of his drink.

"Miss York is still sleeping soundly," Michelle told him in a low tone. "I checked in her on after I finished up in the surgery."

"How is your partner taking the news?"

"I had to sedate her." Michelle sighed. "A mild one, but enough to send her off to dreamland. She gets herself so worked up over things that she can't control. She always has. This isn't the first time I've had to slip something to her to help her sleep." Her mouth twitched into a smile at that. "She should sleep right through until morning. Just like Miss York will."

"And then what do we do?"

"I've phoned the mainland with word of the accident. No response came back to me though...just got the bloody answering service." She shrugged. "So now we wait. I mean, what else can we do?"

Ivan took a sip of his drink. "So what killed him?"

"I'm not sure actually. I told you, my surgery isn't very well equipped. It was never meant for such duties." She shivered. "I found marks on what was left of his flesh. Signs of something tearing and pulling. It wasn't a big animal, I don't think. Certainly not a jaguar or something like that."

"Not that we have jaguars on this island."

"Course not. Orpheus is quite devoid of dangerous animals. We wouldn't have built the resort here if there was a risk like that for the guests."

"What kind of animal could it have been then?"

"I have no idea." Michelle took the drink from Jamie and remained quiet until he had moved back to the other end of the bar. "There aren't any dangerous animals on this island. We would have encountered them long before this."

"That should relieve Shelia."

"She's going to worry herself into a sickbed over this."

"Well, this resort is her dream."

Michelle nodded. "It always was. When I first met in her in that dance club in Melbourne she told me about how she wanted to open a private resort."

"I am trying to picture you in a dance club."

"I used to dance." Michelle giggled and settled more heavily into her chair. "I used to have men and women alike lined up, asking to dance with me. Well, some men at least. Depended on the bar of course."

"And now you have your dream."

"The resort was her dream. Becoming a doctor was mine and I've had years of practice at it. This is a nice place to retire too. Having a doctor on staff is a status marker, you know."

"I'll take your word for it." Ivan shook his head.

Chapter Seven

"I never dreamed that I would be here." Lily gestured to the restaurant they were sitting in. She was pale-faced and shaking slightly as she stumbled through the lobby and into the small restaurant. She wasn't wearing make-up and her hair was only pushed back with a clip holding it in place. "Just look at me. Sitting at a table in a dyke-owned hotel having breakfast with an old lover."

"Shelia and Michelle are a wonderful couple." Ivan shrugged, fighting the urge to take her in his arms again. "You just have to get to know them."

"I can't stay here. Not now. I have to get away."

"No one is going anywhere in this weather." The storm had come up suddenly and the wind and rain were far too violent for any of the boats to venture away from the harbour. "The authorities will be here in the morning."

Lily idly pushed the pieces of fresh fruit around her plate. She sipped some of her juice, but she really wasn't in a mood for food. "I don't need publicity like this, Ivan. I don't want to be splashed over the tabloids."

"Why would you? You didn't kill Simon. It was some animal."

"What kind of animal?" Lily asked. "I didn't see or hear anything! I was there the whole time! He just stepped off the trail and then when I went looking, he was...." Her voice trailed off and she hastily dabbed at her eyes. "God, Ivan, what happened to him?"

"I don't know."

"He didn't want to come here. He had no desire to fly to Australia, let alone take the boat out to this island. I wanted to come. I heard all sorts of fantastic stories about this place from Jackie and Su-lin Yueng when I was filming with her. Su-lin raved about the beaches and the view and how nice the water was."

"Well, it is nice."

"Simon just rolled his eyes at the idea. I made him come here with me. He'd rather have been back in L.A. clubbing and drinking with the rest of celebrity society. I badgered him into this trip. But now Simon's dead."

Ivan grimaced at her tone. "I'd forgotten how much you enjoy your little dramas."

"What?" Her eyes flashed. "How can you say that?" she demanded.

"It's true, isn't it?"

"I have every good reason to be dramatic."

"You overreact about just about anything. You always did."

"Something killed my boyfriend!" Lily took a deep breath and lowered her voice. No one else in the room appeared to notice her outburst. "And you're sitting there accusing me of being overly dramatic?"

"I'm sorry I ever opened my mouth."

"On that note, I agree with you." She stood up. "I'm going to another table. Leave me the hell alone!"

Ivan watched her stomp across the floor.

More rain splattered against the windows.

"Such passion!" Luciano commented in his thickly accented voice. He was seated at one of the tables, with two young woman sharing his bottle of wine. "I love storms...there's something just so raw and primal in it. Can you not feel the passion, Melanie?"

"Oh, I can feel it." She snuggled up closer, leaning against him. "I can really feel it."

Lily walked past the table, holding her half-empty drink. She ignored the Italian and his girlfriend and kept walking towards the bar where Jamie was standing and talking softly with a couple of the other guests.

"The storm is not letting up," the bartender was saying.

"At least it's coming up on the end of typhoon season." Sylvester Rhodes looked at his wife.

Petunia nodded her head. "Thank God for that. It must be simply awful to be stuck here—marooned!—when a real storm comes through."

"It's not so bad," Jamie assured her. He kept his voice calm and gentle. "The resort is built like a rock. There hasn't been a storm yet that could shift us."

Further down the bar, Michelle had poured herself another rum-and-coke and peered glumly at the half-empty restaurant. "No one is going to take a boat out in this weather. Not just to come and collect a body."

"But we'll need a boat to get back to Brisbane." Lily stared at her and she moved closer to the older woman. "They must understand that. We need a boat."

"No one will be coming or going until that storm lets up."

"We need to send Simon home."

"He's perfectly all right where he is." Michelle kept her voice soft and low. "The freezer is more than large enough to keep him."

Lily grimaced. "You put him in the *freezer*?"

"We leave him out, and he'd spoil in this heat. Don't worry, I wrapped him in some plastic and there's plenty of space in the freezer."

Lily stood up and ran from the restaurant.

Michelle watched her run, her mouth hanging open. She caught Ivan's gaze and he shrugged, looking uncomfortable.

* * *

Ivan let himself out into the storm. The wind was howling now, and he could hear the waves splashing against the jetty. Rain was running off the roof of the veranda in a steady curtain. "No one is going anywhere in this." He turned back and stepped back into the hotel.

Shelia was watching him from behind the front desk.

Ivan looked at her and shook his head.

"Has it stopped?"

"No, Lily." He eyed her, but right now she looked calmer than she had at the most uncomfortable breakfast. "It's still raining."

She stepped out of the corridor and moved closer to him, across the lobby. "How much longer?"

"The storm could last for days."

"Days?"

"Could be weeks even." Shelia shrugged and then made a credible attempt at laughter. "Likely blow over by morning though."

"I can't wait!" Lily moved towards the door.

Ivan reached for her arm, but she pushed past.

Lily pulled the door open and stepped out onto the veranda.

"Come back inside!" Shelia called out. "Don't go out there in this!"

Lily vanished into the night.

"Come back!" Shelia shouted.

"Damn idiot girl!" Ivan hurried after her.

The trees were bent almost double by some of the wind gusts.

"This is awful weather." Ivan's clothing was already soaked through and the rain was growing worse. "Stupid girl. Stupid me for following her." He couldn't see far in the darkness and the rain. "Stupid. Stupid. Stupid." He stumbled in the sand.

Ivan heard a scream.

"What the hell?"

Lily staggered out of the rain. "Crabs!" she shouted. "They're everywhere."

"What?"

"They're swarming everywhere!"

Ivan grabbed her arm. "Watch where you're going!" he said. "You could fall and hurt yourself."

"We've got to get off this island!"

The wind was picking up again and he raised his voice to shout over it. "We can't leave in this storm." He reached for her hand. "Come on." He pulled her towards his home.

Ivan closed the door of his cottage and locked it. For some reason, he felt better after doing so, even though he knew it was silly. He undid the buttons on his shirt and pulled it off. He hung it on a hook to drip. His legs were soaked, but his shorts would dry out soon enough. He kicked off his sandals and then turned to his unexpected guest.

Lily was soaked through.

Ivan froze, uncertain how to continue.

"Those damned crabs," Lily muttered. She was staring through the window at the storm. "They're everywhere."

"I'll get you a towel." He pulled his eyes away from her top—the thin cotton had gone transparent and was clinging tightly to her chest.

She looked around, taking in the room with a quick glance. "Small place."

"It does well enough for me." He stepped out of the bathroom, holding a jade green towel. "What more do I need?" he asked. His swung-arm gesture took in the open room with a small kitchenette against one wall, the living space, and his bed in a back corner. "I don't need a lot of space and walls just block the breeze."

"Not much privacy either."

"No one here bothers much with privacy. Just the mainlanders."

"Mainlanders." She shook her head, taking the towel from him. "And just how long have you been living out here to look down everyone else? You're hardly one of the island-born natives."

"There aren't any island-born natives. This was an uninhabited island when the resort was built."

"Oh."

"There are too many laws about building on occupied islands. Anyway, most of the guests prefer tropical resorts with privacy and no concerns. No chance of theft or murders out here." Ivan bit his tongue too late.

Lily stared at him.

Lily stepped out of the bathroom. She was wearing a baggy tee-shirt and cut-off jeans. They were Ivan's clothes, of course, and too large for her, but at least they were dry. Her own clothes were hanging on a hook.

She walked slowly past his desk. "You still write?"

"Of course. I write lots of great fantasy stuff...problem is no one reads it."

Lily picked up a bundle of papers. "This reads like your style," she said after skimming the top page. "But it's pretty trashy."

"Smut sells." Ivan shrugged and tried to make his tone a bit less defensive. "It's what people are buying. I have to cater to what the market wants."

"So you write classic fantasy for fun and you earn a living with your erotica?"

"Yeah." He nodded. "Got a problem with that?"

"No, of course not." Lily shook her head. She already knew that was how he'd been writing since they first got together. "I thought something might have changed."

"Good. I seem to recall a certain actress who dreamed of Oscar-worthy roles...and who bought herself a Hollywood mansion after the second instalment of the *Jungle Jane* series."

Lily looked at him coldly. "I seem to recall a hack writer providing one of the first scripts for that series."

"True." Ivan poured himself a drink. "You want one?"

"Good God yes."

He poured a second rum-and-coke. "It's going to be a fun evening if we can't get along for more than an hour."

"Why is it we always strike sparks from one another?"

"Good question."

Ivan sat down on the bed beside her. "We had a good thing once."

"Yeah, once." Lily shook her head sadly. "That was a long time ago."

"A lifetime."

"Yeah."

Lily looked at her refilled drink. "How strong did you make this?" she asked before taking a sip.

"Strong enough," Ivan replied.

She laughed softly. "I think you're trying to get me drunk. You just want to get into my pants."

"I never had to get you drunk to get into your pants." Ivan chuckled. "Anyway, right now you're wearing *my* pants."

Wetting her bottom lip with her tongue, she stood up and then half-walked, half-staggered towards him but she stopped just out of his reach. Her eyes were sparkling with mischief. "Ivan," she said. "Ivan." She sighed loudly. "Why did we break up?"

"Because we were both to damned strong-willed." Ivan stared at her. "What are you doing?"

She was very slowly, and very deliberately, lifting up the hem of her tee-shirt, pulling it over her head, tossing it gracefully onto the floor. Her hands moved down to the button of her cut-offs.

Ivan licked his own lips as he listened to the slow rasp of the zipper sliding down. His own shorts were bulging outwards. "You need to stop," he said.

"No, I don't." She shook her head. "I need you right now." She kicked the jeans away to land in a heap with her discarded shirt.

Ivan stared at her. "Damn it!" He swore under his breath and began stripping off his own clothes, almost ripping them off in his desperation.

They embraced and kissed.

They tumbled into the bed, rolling in the sheets.

Ivan reached for the drawer of his nightstand and pulled it open. As hard as he was, rolling a condom on was a painful exercise in self discipline. "Oh god, Lily." He leaned forward and opened his mouth over hers, kissing her.

As she gasped, he drove into her with one hard stroke, closing his eyes at the erotic feel of her flesh gripping him so tightly. He kept his mouth fastened to hers, his tongue plundering the warm cavern inside with strokes in time to those of his manhood as he rocked her back against the wall. He felt her hard nipples pressing into his chest and her nails digging into his skin as she clutched his shoulders.

Chapter Eight

Silence.

Lily opened her eyes. The night was quiet...the storm had finally blown itself out. Moonlight was shining brightly through the windows.

Lily rolled over.

Ivan was laying next to her. His eyes were closed and he was breathing deeply as he slept.

She blinked, suddenly remembering where she was, and then gasped. "Oh." She scrambled to her feet, clutching at one of the sheets as she realized she was naked.

Ivan opened his eyes. "Morning." He blinked blearily, and glanced at his wristwatch. "It's way too early to get up."

"I—I've got to get back to the hotel."

"It's four in the morning."

"I can 't stay here." Lily shook her head. "I can't. This was a mistake." She wrapped the sheets more tightly pulled around herself. "You and I are not an item. We broke up for a good reason. I can't stay here. Simon is—I can't—"

"Lily—"

"This was a mistake." Lily could hear the raw emotions in her voice as she kept shaking her head in denial. "My God, Simon was killed yesterday and then last night you and I—you took advantage—I made a mistake coming here."

Ivan was sitting up now. One of the sheets was covering him to his waist, leaving his chest and torso bare. He didn't speak.

Lily tore her eyes away from his tanned body. "It's stopped raining. I should get dressed and go back to our—my—room."

"You can stay here til morning."

"No, I shouldn't." Lily snatched up her clothes and darted into the bathroom.

"Those will still be wet!" Ivan called out. "You can put my tee and shorts back on."

"These will be fine." Lily opened the bathroom door and stepped back out into the living room. Her clothes were damp and the shirt clung to her breasts. "It's not far."

"I'll escort you."

"No!" Lily waved at him to stay seated. "Don't bother. It's not all that far." She reached for the door and opened it. "Oh my God!" she screamed.

"What?"

"Outside!"

Ivan swung his legs out of bed and stumbled naked to the doorway and peered out.

The patio was moving.

"Crabs." He swore. "Thousands of them."

"Why are they here?" Lily backed away from the door. "Why are they doing this?"

"They're just animals," Ivan said. "You can't expect them to be doing this from some plan."

The sound was just loud enough to hear, soft clicking sounds of shells scraping against one other as the swarm scuttled along the ground.

"They sure seem to be organized."

Ivan watched the crabs climbing up his patio chairs and table. They really were *everywhere*. "It's all just random. It has to be." He closed the door and locked it again. "That will keep them out."

Lily was shaking.

Ivan hurried to the window in the kitchenette. "Yep, they're over here too." He flicked his finger against the screen, knocking two crabs loose. Then he closed the window and locked it. "Did I leave any other windows open?" He didn't think so.

"Can't you call for help?"

"From who?"

"Someone at the hotel."

Ivan shrugged. "No phone."

Lily whirled around to face him. "No phone? How can you not have a phone?"

"Never wanted one. Don't believe in the damned things. Part of the resort's charm is the lack of decent cell-phone coverage."

"It works at the hotel."

"Because you're tied into the hotel's service. I think Shelia pays for a direct satellite up-link. Same with the internet connection." Ivan gave her a casual shrug. "I'm not sure about that though."

"You always were so old fashioned." Lily turned and gestured at the cluttered desk top. "You have that lap-top."

"Easier to write and edit on it. I can type almost as fast as I think up new material. Pen and paper can't keep up with me."

"You edit your work on paper."

"True." He nodded. "Always have done. Seems to work better for me that way."

Lily sighed. "So how long can we stay here?"

"I've got enough supplies to stay here a good month or more." He gestured to one of the doors. "The pantry is partially underground, in case of a good typhoon, so I don't have to run to the hotel every single day."

"You've been there most of the last week."

"I was helping Shelia with some painting in a few guests rooms. Good manager, hopeless with a paint brush."

"Oh."

"Anyway, it's nice to go there and visit. The resort has better chefs." Ivan chuckled. "We'll have no shortage of power for the lights. Solar panels on the roof and lots of battery storage."

"How efficient."

"It's always sunny down here...why waste it?" The moonlight faded and fresh rain splashed against the windows. "Okay, mostly always sunny."

Lily looked at him.

"Come back to bed," he told her softly. "You need sleep. I'll take you back to the hotel tomorrow."

* * *

The tropical sun was shining and the air was muggy.

"I need air conditioning." Lily was fanning her face with her hand.

"It's no worse than L.A."

"Yes, it is. The humidity is just..."

"It was the storm. It will clear out in a bit." Ivan shook his head and walked across the sand towards the hotel. "Let's see if Shelia has that boat ready yet."

"G'day." Michelle waved at them from the veranda. She was looking tired. "I see that you found her after all That's good news. We could use a bit of that right now."

"Oh?"

"Shelia's not taking any of this very well."

"I don't blame her." Ivan opened the door and stepped into the lobby.

Shelia was just stepping out of her office and she spotted them. "Ivan. Miss York."

Lily said nothing.

Michelle closed the door behind her.

"Things are getting worse."

Ivan looked at Shelia, frowning at the sound of her voice. "How much worse?"

"No one has seen Donny or Betty in *two* days."

"Two days?"

"I've taken a poll of my staff. They've been gone for two days."

Ivan frowned. "That's...."

"Worrisome." Michelle shook her head. "No one has seen them, Ivan. Jamie said he had last served them two night ago. They were talking about going off for a midnight swim."

"How romantic."

"But they don't appear to have come back," Shelia continued. "Their bed wasn't slept in. They haven't come to the bar and they certainly haven't called for room service."

"No food, no water, and outside in that storm?" Ivan grimaced. "This is a recipe for disaster."

"I know. Do you think they drowned?" Shelia asked. "Or could they have ended up like Simon?"

Lily gasped.

"We still don't know what happened to Simon."

"I have some ideas though."

Michelle darted a glance at Ivan.

"The crabs," he said.

"Crabs?"

"Yes, Shelia. We keep seeing them around at night. They're swarming unlike anything I've seen. Thousands of them at a time."

"The ground is literally covered," Lily said in a low tone. "I was watching them from my balcony. And then last night outside Ivan's cottage...."

Shelia slumped down into a wingback chair. There were half a dozen of those chairs in the lobby. "This place was my dream, you know. I wanted to open a resort and enjoy the islands. I talked Michelle into it. I sank my life savings into this place. All the inheritance I got from my grandparents. I could have had any kind of life I wanted, but I chose this."

Michelle patted her shoulder. "You're doing a fine job running the resort"

"I've built a death trap!" Shelia gave a start and looked around, but no one else was in the lobby to overheard her outburst. "I'm just not ready for this."

"How can anyone be ready for a crab swarm?"

"What can we do?"

"I don't know."

"First thing we do is not panic," Michelle said firmly. "We don't want to alarm the other guests."

"We have to tell them! We can't risk anyone out getting killed."

"Of course not."

Shelia shook her head. "What can I say?"

Michelle looked at Ivan. "We'll think of something."

* * *

Ivan nodded to Jasmine as he walked past her.

The maid gave him a nervous smile.

"What's wrong?" he asked. *As if I didn't already know.*

"The hotel is...sad." Jasmine was moving slowly this morning. She was pushing a supply-laden cart in front of her. "Just my arthritis," she said. "Always bad after a storm."

"You should take a rest then."

"After my work is done." Jasmine chuckled. "I don't have time to lay around...I'm not on vacation."

Ivan laughed along with it. *Jamie, Jasmine, and Alison.* The resort only had a small staff, Ivan noted. He'd helped out on occasion with the odd chore when they became overwhelmed. "Sad because of Simon's death?"

"And two other guests are missing. The ladies are sad."

"I know." Ivan nodded. *'The ladies'* always referred to Shelia and Michelle.

"And the guests are afraid to leave their rooms."

"They shouldn't be in any danger indoors. The crabs are just acting strangely right now."

"I know. I'm not afraid to walk around inside the resort." Jasmine tapped her supply cart. "But you won't catch me down on the beach."

Ivan couldn't blame her.

Chapter Nine

"Lily, what are you doing?"

"Trying to find a safe place."

"There is nowhere safe out here." Ivan looked around past the railing of the veranda. "Just a whole lot of crabs." The ground was a living carpet of red shells. "We'll never reach the jetty." He could see it, plainly enough, and the resort's boats bobbing in the water. *But they're too far away for us to reach.*

Lily was eyeing the boats as well. "Can't we push them back? Sweep them with brooms or something?"

"I don't think the hotel fire hoses have the pressure to be a water cannon."

"We can't stay here."

"Of course we can." Ivan gestured. "The hotel is secure. We have plenty of food and water. Shelia has called the mainland again. Someone will come to rescue us."

"You hope."

"Someone will come." He paused for a moment. "Now why don't you come back inside with me?"

"I like the feel of the breeze."

"Those crabs are moving again."

Lily looked down. She hastily took a step backwards and small pincers snipped at her sandal-clad feet.

The crabs were moving forward again, their claws waving in the air.

"How do we get out of this?"

"I have no clue." Ivan rubbed at his chin. "This isn't like anything I've ever seen before," he protested.

A loud splash sounded from just around the corner of the resort.

Ivan frowned. "What the hell?"

"Good God!" Lily screamed.

The crab was a real monster as it scuttled over a decorative boulder and into their view. The slowly waving claws had a span easily more than three feet wide.

Ivan bit off a curse. "It's got to be twenty-five pounds or more!" It was huge—he'd never seen a crab that size before.

The crab scuttled forward.

"It's coming this way."

"I know." Ivan nodded. "Now we run."

Michelle and Shelia looked up from the table top as the lobby door slammed closed. "What the—"

"We've got a problem." Ivan leaned against the closed door, gasping for breath. "A bigger one than we thought."

"Bigger than the crab swarm?"

"Oh yeah." Lily staggered to one of the wingback chairs and collapsed into it. "A lot bigger."

"Keep the door locked!" Ivan said. "There's a monster out there."

"A monster?" Michelle was frowning as she looked at them. "Have the two of you been drinking?"

"Not yet," Ivan told her. "We just saw a monster crab in the garden. It's the size of a small horse."

"Another monster?" Shelia shook her head. "This just gets better and better, doesn't it?"

"We need to do something."

"You'll get no argument from me, but what do you suggest?"

Ivan cleared his throat. "When can we expect help to arrive from the mainland?"

Shelia shook her head. "I still can't get through."

"What?"

"I can't get a connection," Shelia told Lily in a grim voice. "The receiver is down."

Ivan grimaced. "So we're cut off?"

"For now."

"We're *cut* off?" Lily's voice was quite loud. "A swarm of killer crabs is out there and we're trapped on an island?"

"They're just crabs."

"There's thousands of them out there, luv." Michelle stepped away from the window, a frown on her face. "We'd be snipped to pieces before we can reach the boat."

"Jamie, go and make sure that all of the doors and windows are locked. I don't want any of them getting in here."

The blond bartender nodded. "I'm on it."

A dull thump sounded from the door.

"Now they're knocking to come in." Lily shook her head. "This is insane."

"It looks like a Kamchatka," Shelia commented as she looked through the window. "A Red King Crab."

"How do you know that?"

"I like sea food. Kamchatka are a speciality. It's legs are considered a delicacy and fetch a really pretty price in Japan and America. Goes for about fifteen pounds a pound...of course, a single leg will feed a grown man."

"I'd hate to be the fisherman who has to go after one of them."

"Divers do it."

Lily was shaking her head. "They could snip off a finger with those claws!"

"Or worse."

"I think," Michelle said in a low tone of voice, "that we have found Simon's killer."

Ivan looked at her. "You think it was one of them?"

"It seems likely. They'll eat just about anything from what I recall."

"Even us?"

"Possibly."

* * *

Lily was staring at the closed door. Her face was very pale and her eyes were wide and unblinking. "What are the odds on us surviving this horror movie disaster?"

Ivan sipped at a beer. "Good question."

"We're safe enough indoors." Shelia peered through a window, and then slowly walked back to the bar. "There's enough food in the pantry to last us a few months."

"Months?" Lily asked. She had refused to be left alone.

"I like to be prepared for anything." Shelia chuckled. "But we have a supply boat come out every week or so. Top up the essentials, bring new guests, take other guests back to the mainland unless other arrangements were made." Then she shrugged. "Byron will be here in two days."

"I'm still surprised that no one has tried calling us."

"It happens sometimes, Lily. The satellite must be down."

"You should check your emails," Ivan said to Michelle. "Just in case."

"If the net was down for any real length of time, we'd have gotten complaints from the other guests," she replied. "No one has called down to complain."

"So it could be a natural thing."

"Could...could *they* have cut a line?"

Ivan shook his head. "They're just animals."

"The transmitter is on the eastern peak of the roof. If they could climb up there, they'd be swarming us through the windows by now." Michelle forced a laugh from her lips. "Or we'd have them in the vents."

* * *

"We should make a run for the docks." Jamie made that comment in a soft voice. He was sipping a beer.

"The boats?" Ivan asked.

"If we could get away from the shore, out to see, then we'd be okay." Lily looked around the table. They were the only people in the restaurant. "Wouldn't we?"

Ivan shrugged. "Depends on how hungry those beasts are. They might ignore us..." his voice trailed off for a moment before he continued, "and they might swarm us."

Lily swallowed hard. "Simon," she whispered.

"The boats are there," Jamie pointed out. "We cast off and we're safe."

"You want us to sail back to the mainland in a skimmer?" Ivan asked him.

Jamie shrugged. "There's a speedboat tied up."

"When the hell did the ladies buy a speedboat?"

Jamie laughed. "It belongs to one of the guests. Luciano."

"The old guy?"

"Yeah."

Ivan looked round the restaurant. "And where is Luciano?"

"Probably in his room." Jamie coughed into his hand. He lowered his voice. "With Victoria or Melanie. Or both," he finished.

Ivan stared at him.

Jamie shrugged, a grin on his face. "They called for room service one time."

"I see."

Jamie gave him a leer. "I got a special tip for that delivery."

"I bet you did."

"It was worth the trip up." Jamie stood up and pushed his chair away from the table. "I'll go up to the room and talk to Luciano."

"Do that. I'll give some thoughts how we can reach the boats."

Chapter Ten

"Has anyone seen Jamie?"

"No."

Ivan frowned as he gave thought to that. "Not since this morning," he admitted. "We were talking in the restaurant. He was going to talk to Luciano about us making use of his speedboat."

"I can't find him." Michelle kept her voice low as she leaned over the table. "Alison is missing too."

"The cook and the bartender are off together?" Ivan bit off a laugh. "I didn't think he was into older women."

"Neither did I. But I can't find either of them right now."

"Damn." Ivan bit his lip. "We'll have to search the resort."

"I already checked their rooms."

"Did you find his surfboard?"

"Ivan! You can't think he would go surfing at a time like this!"

"Nothing he might do would surprise me. He's not the brightest guy around."

"He's a good worker."

"And a good flirt. Ever watch him around the young women?"

"He never crossed the line," she snapped.

Ivan bit his tongue.

"I made it very clear what sort of behaviour Shelia and I expect from our staff," Michelle told him. "While on duty or when off. Especially when off-duty. No one has ever complained."

"I doubt he gave them a reason too. What happens while on vacation...."

Michelle snorted. "Why not talk about you and Miss York? Did *that* stay on vacation?"

"That relationship was a long time ago."

"So you and she have—"

"She came here with a new boyfriend, Michelle. Remember him?"

"Yes! Of course I do!" Michelle wiped her hand across her face. "I'm sorry, Ivan, I'm just a bit...stressed."

He looked away from her for a moment. "I'm sorry too. We're all feeling the strain now."

"Shelia and I are under a lot of pressure right now. Guests are missing and we've already found one body. What if the others are..."

Ivan gripped her arm with his hand. "Don't jump to conclusions."

"We need to get off this island."

"I know. That was what Jamie was up too the last I saw of him. He was going to talk to Luciano about his boat."

"So what did Luciano say?"

"I never heard...Jamie went off on his own. And now you say he's vanished?"

"Yes."

Ivan looked through the window. "I can't see the dock from here."

"You think they made a run for the boat and left us?"

"I can't see that. Not Jamie. They might have gone out to look at it," Ivan guessed. "If they made it through the crabs once, they might not have wanted to try and fight their way through the swarm a second time."

"They'll send us help."

Ivan heard the desperate hope in Michelle's voice.

"Of course they will." He couldn't imagine them having done anything else.

* * *

"They're still out there." Lily turned away from the window with a shudder. "Thousands of them. They're swarming over everything." She glanced across the room at Ivan.

He was sitting in a chair, sipping on a drink.

"Thank God they're all the small ones. I don't think I could handle a swarm made up entirely of the large ones."

"Calm down," Ivan said. "Have a drink or something." He looked around, but none of the other patrons in the restaurant were paying much attention.

Michelle and Shelia walked into the restaurant. "All the doors are locked up tighter than a drum," Michelle told them. "So are all the windows."

"We can outlast them." Shelia was a bit unsteady on her feet. "No need to panic."

"No need to panic?" Lily exclaimed. "Those monsters have killed or eaten four people!" Her voice was rising. "At least four."

Michelle made a *shushing* sound.

"And they're outside and we're safe inside," Shelia pointed out.

The elderly couple looked up from their table. The plate of food in front of them was barely touched.

Lily laughed bitterly. "They have us trapped."

Jasmine set a plate down onto the table and then sat down next to them. "I've been taking a poll," she announced, "and we're missing more guests."

"More guests?" Shelia said. "This is an island...they can't have simply wandered off."

"Hush," Michelle told her. "Who's missing now?"

"Betty and Donny, as we already knew. Jamie has buggered off. Allison might have gone with him...I've caught the two of them fooling around in the pantry on more than one occasion. Worse than two teenagers they were."

Ivan blinked at that piece of news.

Shelia was muttering darkly under her breath.

"Luciano Pederzani is missing as well. So are those nice two girls. Victoria Reeve and Melanie Chambers. They spent a lot of time with Luciano."

Shelia shook her head. "This is a disaster. A terrible disaster..."

"We can't stay here," Ivan said. "We have to reach the boats."

"But how can we do that?"

"Animals hate fire." Ivan stood up with a grin on his face.

"So?" Michelle prompted.

"If we made some torches, we might be able to keep them back long enough to reach the docks."

"And grab ourselves a boat?"

"And grab ourselves a boat." Ivan nodded his agreement. "Assuming that they're fuelled."

Shelia had lowered her head onto the table.

"I gave her something to steady her nerves," Michelle explained to Ivan in a soft voice. "She's a bit out of it right now."

"Great."

"I don't know if the boats are fuelled," Michelle added. "Jamie was supposed to be looking after them. I—I don't know how much he got done."

"So we might reach the docks and we might end up trapped."

"If nothing else, we cast off and hope the current catches us."

"And washes us out to sea? I'd sooner take my chances locked in here." Ivan was frowning. "I wish we could find out."

"One way or the other?"

"Exactly."

"I am too old to run," Jasmine told them. She had a half-eaten grilled cheese sandwich on her plate. "I'll break a hip."

"Then shove her in her supply cart and we can push her to the boat." Michelle gave her a smile. "Will that work?"

"Yes, thank you, dear."

Ivan was looking at himself. "I need some other clothes to wear. Shorts won't give me any protection."

Michelle shook her head. "You can't go outside like that. You'll never reach your cottage to change."

"No, I won't."

"You can use Simon's clothes." Lily spoke up from where she was sitting. "He brought three suitcases with him. There should be something in there that would be suitable."

"Three suitcases?" Ivan asked as they walked along the hallway. "What was he expecting?"

"He likes—liked—to have a variety of things ready to wear. He was never sure what the weather would bring." Lily laughed softly. "The day before we left for the airport, he had enough clothes out to fill ten suitcases. It took him half the day to trim down to what he called 'the barest essentials.'"

Ivan shook his head. "I don't think I could fill three suitcases with every last thing I own."

"That's not surprising."

He glanced at her. "Orpheus is a tropical island. Shorts, tee-shirts, swim trunks, some slacks and dressier shirts just in case...that pretty much covers it."

"Not like back in Hollywood?"

"Hell no. I haven't worn a suit in years. There are hardly any parties held here. No hectic social calendar to keep up and God forbid you show up to events in the same outfit." He shook his head with a grimace. "I'm glad to be rid of that."

"You looked nice when you wore that suit to the premiere of *Jungle Jane and the Lost City*."

"I felt uncomfortable the whole night."

"You looked...good," Lily finally finished.

Ivan looked at her.

Lily reached for the door to her room. "I'll get you those clothes."

Ivan followed her into the room.

"Jeans are over in the wardrobe. Bottom drawer." She pointed.

Ivan nodded his head. "Shelia got a deal on bulk furniture for this place. Every room has the same set of furnishings."

"Nothing wrong with that. Guests only use one room after all. I don't many of them go from room to room to compare the furniture." Lily opened the closet door and pulled out a brown leather jacket. "This should give you lots of protection."

Ivan was staring at her. He had a pair of blue jeans, still neatly folded, in his hands.

"You should wear the jacket."

"Why the hell did he bring a leather jacket to a tropical island?"

"He wore it everywhere he went. He brought it in case it got cold." She laughed at that. "A tropical island and he was afraid of getting cold."

Ivan tossed the jeans onto the bed. He dropped his shorts and let them slide down his legs.

Lily was staring at him.

"Like what you see?"

"I've seen it before."

Ivan turned towards the bed and bent over to pick up the jeans. His boxer briefs clung to the curves of his legs and hips. "We should get going."

Lily leaned close and gave him a kiss on his cheek.

"What was that for?"

"You look like you could use it."

"Thanks."

"So..." Lily was staring at him.

"So?" he prompted.

"Be safe out there." She leaned in close to him. "I don't want to lose you." Their bodies fit together perfectly. Chest to chest, groin to groin, and thigh to thigh. The front of his underwear was bulging outwards, ready to burst, and his hardness was hot against her leg.

Ivan let the jeans fall to the floor.

Lily leaned into him even more. His arms were wrapped around her, his hands were running through her hair, his lips were on her neck. She gripped his head and pulled him back, so she could nuzzle her head under his chin. She licked up the side of his neck, felt the rasp of stubble against her tongue, and tasted the slightly salty flavor of man.

He could only groan softly.

She rubbed against him, feeling the rigid length of his manhood burn into her belly through their clothes.

Ivan's hand ran down her back and cupped her ass, pulling her even tighter against him as their lips met again in an open-mouthed, hungry kiss.

Lily struggled to breathe, to think. Her breasts ached, bolts of pleasure zinging through her every time she rubbed against his bare chest. But it wasn't enough.

Her fingers danced lightly across his bulge, and then she gripped the waistband and yanked his boxer briefs down past his knees.

He sprang free.

Lily smiled at his groan.

"Lily," he said softly, "we shouldn't do this."

"Yes, we should." She leaned forward and let her breath tease him. She ran her hands up and down his thighs—those lovely muscled thighs that had made her drool from the first minute she'd met him. They were thick and corded with the muscle of a man who worked at staying strong. There was a light brown layer of fur that covered them. Softer than the hair of any man she'd met.

She put her hands between his legs and pushed them apart, widening his stance, then leaned in and licked her way up his inner thigh. She could hear his gasp and his panting breath echo in the quiet room, and her own fire burned hotter.

"Oh God, Lily!" Ivan's fingers tightened in her hair and she smiled against his skin.

Chapter Eleven

Ivan stepped through the doorway into the lobby.

"You look like a biker." Shelia laughed loudly.

Iva shook his head. "At least I should have some protection from the crabs," he told them. "Is there a torch?"

"Yes," Michelle was holding a long stick, wrapped with cloth.

Ivan eyed it. "An umbrella?"

"What else do you suggest we use?" Michelle asked.

Lily followed him towards the door. "You'll send help back for us, won't you?"

"I don't plan to leave any of you behind. I'm going to check the boat and see if it's seaworthy. Then I'll come back and we'll figure out how to get everyone there."

Lily leaned in close to him. "Hurry back."

"I will." Ivan eyed her.

Michelle unlatched the door and then swung it open.

The veranda was devoid of crabs for the moment, but the patio was covered with a living carpet of crabs.

Ivan light the end of the torch watched it burn and smoke for a moment, then he lowered the torch and waved it back and forth.

The crabs scuttled away from him.

With a muffled curse, Ivan swung the torch again.

Lily was watching from the doorway.

Michelle had her own torch and she was keeping the doorway clear. "Hurry up!"

Ivan waved.

"Stay safe!" Lily called.

Ivan walked along the veranda, keeping close to the building for as long as he could. The canopy was providing enough shelter to keep crabs from falling down on him.

He eyed the jetty and the boats bouncing on the waves there. It would be a quick jog.

A patio chair fell over with a thump.

Ivan turned his head.

One of the Kamchatka crabs was advancing on him.

Ivan's mouth went dry. "Damn." This particular specimen was easily three feet across. The claws were waving slowly, as if the crab was still underwater.

The monster crab snapped at him.

Ivan thrust his torch towards it, like a sword.

The crab hissed and backed away.

"Get away!" Ivan snapped.

The Kamchatka snapped at him again.

"Ivan?" Lily called out.

"Stay inside!" he shouted. He kept waving the torch at the beast.

"But—"

"Stay inside!"

The Kamchatka backed away.

Ivan ran for the dock, leaving the hotel behind. The crabs were really thick around the shoreline—every step he took sounded with a crunch—and he was forced to slow down and pick his way carefully. The torch drove the crabs back, but only a few feet and the hole filled right back in.

He walked around the corner of a low wall and planter.

A body was laying on the ground, crabs swarming over it.

Ivan winced. It was Jamie—what flesh he could see had the surfer's bronze tan and the head was covered with blond hair. "Damn."

The boat was bobbing gently on the waves. It was tied to the dock with a few ropes. It didn't look like there were any crabs around.

"Hello?" Ivan called out. "Luciano?" There was no answer.

Ivan looked around again, but there were only a few crabs. A dozen or so at most. Slowly, Ivan climbed aboard.

The deck was deserted.

The cabin door was closed.

Ivan tried the handle. It was locked. He pulled at it again. "Hello?" He waited, but no one responded.

Ivan moved to the rail and stood eyeing the distant resort.

It looked peaceful.

He heard a soft thud as the hull bounced against the jetty.

"We could just cast off," he said aloud. "We'd drift, but we'd be found sooner or later." He'd had to break the hatch open and see what stores were in the cabin. "We'll grab some food and fresh water before we make our break for it." That seemed like their best hope.

Another soft thud echoed.

Ivan turned. "What the hell is that?" He moved to the other side of the boat and looked over the side.

A body was floating in the water, bumping against the hull.

Male. Greying hair.

"Luciano."

* * *

Lily jumped at a pounding on the door.

Michelle opened it. "Ivan!"

"Who else would be fool enough to go out in this?" He stepped through the door and then closed it. His boots were glistening and shone wetly.

Lily hurried across the foyer and gave Ivan a hug and a kiss. "Welcome back."

"Thanks." Ivan pulled his boots off and left them by the door.

"Did you reach the boat?" Michelle and Shelia were looking at him. "Yeah."

"Did you find the others?"

Ivan's mouth hung open.

"Any sign of Jamie?" Michelle asked. "Or Luciano? Or those two girls?"

"I never saw any trace of the two girls," Ivan told her carefully.

Michelle frowned, and then she grimaced. "Oh."

Lily was still holding onto Ivan's arm. "Is the boat seaworthy?"

"Yeah.. It's fuelled and ready to go. We just have to reach it"

"Good...let's go."

"In a bit. We need to gather up some additional supplies." Ivan slumped into a chair, looking blankly across the lobby. "We're gonna need food and water. I didn't see much of either in the galley."

"No, Luciano didn't carry many supplies with him. Most just enough things to throw a little party out at sea." Shelia nodded, more to herself than to Ivan. "Plenty of stuff in the kitchen we can take though."

"Just grab stuff we can carry," Ivan told her. "Nothing we need to cook. And as much bottled water as you can find."

"I've got plenty of supplies around," she told him.

Michelle laughed at that. "She's ready for Orpheus to be isolated by monsoons or typhoons for a good month or more. You've got enough tins in the larder to last out a war."

Shelia shrugged. "I like being prepared," she said in her defence. "Jasmine always told me—"

Ivan interrupted by clearing his throat. "So where is Jasmine?"

"Oh, she went to round up the other guests. What's left of them."
Shelia looked at the handful of people who were slowly gathering in the
foyer. "She's been gone a long time."

"What other guests? Who's not down here?"

"The older couple. Petunia and Sylvester."

"So where are they?"

"I have no idea."

Ivan bolted to his feet.

Lily let go of his arm. "In their room perhaps."

Ivan sighed. "Let's go get them then. Shelia, you can get the food
ready. And find some more torches." He looked at his boots.

Ivan followed Lily around the corner.

She glanced back at him. "Will we be safe on the boat?"

"Of course," Ivan replied. "The crabs can't swim. They only scuttle
and crawl...once we cut the mooring lines, they won't be able to get
aboard."

"Good...I don't think I could sleep otherwise." She yawned. "When
we got off this island, I am going to sleep for a week."

"Yeah?"

"Yeah. Oh!" Lily pointed. "Look, there's Jasmine's cart."

"Is that Petunia's room?"

"I guess so.'" Lily walked closer. She knocked on the closed door.
"Hello?"

"No answer." Ivan frowned and stepped closer.

"They must be inside." She knocked more loudly. "Petunia?
Sylvester? Jasmine? It's Lily York. We've found a way off the island. Are
you there?" She reached for the doorknob. "Perhaps they're asleep."

The door swung inwards.

"Shit!" Ivan pulled Lily backwards.

He slammed the door.

Ivan leaned against the door, breathing heavily.

"Did—did you see it?" Lily asked in a soft voice. "The—the bed was co—covered with crabs."

"I saw." Ivan nodded.

"And the floor was teeming. And there was a lump on it...a body-sized lump underneath all those crabs."

Something thumped against the door.

Lily let out a scream and jumped back.

Ivan could feel his own heart racing as he backed away from the door. "Let's get back to the foyer," he said.

"Wha—"

"Let's go now."

"How did they get in?"

"Open window maybe." Ivan wasn't sure. *Why didn't they get away? Even the two older couple could have gotten away.*

Lily was shaking. "We're on the second floor!"

"I know that."

The door thumped again.

"Could someone be alive in there?"

"I doubt it." Ivan shook his head. "Not a chance."

"We can't leave someone behind."

Ivan bit off a curse. "Lily!"

She reached for the doorknob. "Hello?"

Thump.

Lily turned the handle.

The door swung open.

"Run!" Ivan yanked her backwards.

One of the huge Kamchatka crabs scuttled into the hallway. Its claws snapped loudly and a veritable red tide of crabs swarmed around its legs.

Lily screamed.

A second Kamchatka appeared in the doorway.

Ivan pushed Jasmine's cart towards the first one. "Run!" He grabbed Lily and pulled her after him. They ran down the hallway.

"We're leaving! Right now!" Ivan snapped as he ran into the lobby. He was dragging Lily behind him.

"What about—"

"They're dead," Ivan said. "Jasmine too. The upper floor is overrun with crabs. Including two of those Kamchatka. At least two."

"Damn." Michelle was holding a bag.

Shelia looked faint.

Andy and Christie exchanged looks.

Ivan eyed the small group. "We're leaving. Right now."

They stepped outside.

Ivan was leading, waving a burning torch to keep the crabs clear of his feet. Lily was following right on his heels. Michelle and Shelia had torches as well, trying to keep an open space around the rest of the group.

Most of the others had torches as well.

"Couldn't we have just stayed inside?" Christie was asking. "We could have kept the doors and windows locked."

Her husband kept hold of her arm.

Lily bit her lip to keep from saying anything.

"We just have to walk through the patio and then down the short walk to the beach and the dock." Ivan kept his voice calm. "We're almost there."

Shelia was staring at one of the flowerbeds. The trees rose overhead, but the flowers had been trampled almost flat. "Look at the mess the bastards made. It's going to take weeks to get this place cleaned up."

"I know," Michelle told her.

"We'll have missed the flowering season entirely."

"I know, dear." Michelle tapped her shoulder. "Come on, we have to get to Luciano's boat."

Shelia wiped her eyes.

Lily walked forward, tiny crabs crunching under every step. She didn't even cringe slightly at the sound.

Ivan glanced back towards her.

She gave him a smile.

Christie let out a piercing scream.

The others turned, startled at the shrieks.

"Andy!" Crabs were falling from the tree branches, landing on her. "Andy!" she screamed again. She had blood on her face and arms.

"Christie!" He moved towards her.

"Knock them off!" Ivan shouted. He stomped at the crabs swarming around his feet. "Damn it!"

Kamchatka scuttled out of the underbrush towards them. Four or five of the monster-sized beasts, with claws waving slowly.

"Keep moving." Ivan thrust his torch at the closest one.

It reared up and snapped its claws at him.

"Get to the dock!" Ivan shouted.

More of the Kamchatka scuttled forward.

"Get away from me!" Shelia smacked the crab with her torch.

"Come on!" Andy pulled on his wife's arm. She staggered after him, blood tricking from dozens of small cuts. She was no longer screaming, her face blank and lacking any expression.

"Shock!" Michelle called out as she reached for his arm. "She'll be fine, Andy, just keep her moving."

Ivan tossed the ring of keys to Lily. "I'll buy you some time."

"But, Ivan!"

"Go!"

The dock was almost hidden beneath tiny crabs.

"Get aboard!" Ivan shouted. He waved the others towards the boat. "Run!" He turned back, waving his torch at the giant crabs.

They ran, crabs crunching under foot.

Lily ran along the wood jetty. The boards rattled under her feet. "We're here, Ivan!" she shouted. "Come on!"

Andy pulled his near-catatonic wife onto the boat.

"Get her down below," Michelle told him. "I'll look at her in a minute."

Ivan was still swinging the torch as he retreated.

More of the Kamchatka were scuttling towards him. Their claws clacked together loudly.

The boat floated away from the dock.

Ivan turned the wheel and aimed the prow towards the open sea. The motor rumbled softly.

"My resort," Shelia said in a soft voice. She was standing at the back of the boat, looking towards Orpheus Island as it receded behind them. "All the guests we lost. Jamie. Jasmine."

"We'll come back and rebuild," Michelle told her. "That swarm won't stay on land forever. They—they'll go back into the ocean eventually."

Lily put her arm around Ivan.

Connect with Me Online:

Smashwords: http://www.smashwords.com/profile/view/MattKirkby

Facebook: http://facebook.com/MattKirkby

Facebook Fan-Page: Matt Kirkby's Facebook fan page

Also by Matt Kirkby

A Novel of Lovecraftian Horror
The Death of Hope

Stories Of Feudal Japan
With Honour Veiled

The Empyrean Republic
Empress of All The Stars

Standalone
A Wyrm In the Heart
Cthonian Dragons
Forlorn Gambit
Reap What Has Been Sown
The Horror From The Sea
Vector Of Infection

About the Author

Born and raised in small-town Ontario, Matt Kirkby is a romantic dreamer who specializes in writing tales of high fantasy and pulp-style science fiction and space operas. He draws his inspiration from all diverse sources and ideas: Science Fiction, Fantasy, Gothic Horror, Pastoral Nature. He started his writing career submitting fan fiction for numerous Star Wars and TransFormers fanzines, but has since moved on to writing professionally. He published his first novel, A Wyrm In The Heart in 2004. He lives a double life, writing classy sci-fi and fantasy for fun under his own name, and penning gay erotica under the pen name of Frank Sol. When not writing, Matt spends his time helping his partner with his hand-crafted rocking chair business -- www.OffYourRocker.ca -- and trying to maintain some control over his cat. He still thinks that no gift is better than a new book.

www.ingramcontent.com/pod-product-compliance
Lightning Source LLC
Chambersburg PA
CBHW031000180726

47993CB00018B/1206